THE PETS YOU GET!

Thomas Taylor
Adrian Reynolds

ANDERSEN PRESS

My sister's got a guinea pig –
A little fuzzy friend.
She loves it 'cause it's cuddly,
And hugs it without end.

But me, I think a guinea pig
Is such a boring pet!
It's nothing like as whiz-bang great
As other pets you get.

Now a dog's more exciting, more fun,
He can bark,
he can **leap**,
he can **run**.

At the beach we'd be **free**,
We would **splash** in the sea,

Then we'd sleep on the sand when we're done.

But Sister says that dogs are smelly
And chew your toys and shoes,

While guinea pigs like watching telly,
And just do tiny poos.

But they can keep their cuddles
And their boring TV set.
If not a dog then never mind,
I know the perfect pet . . .

I would love an **enormous** brown bear,
with **claws**, pointy teeth, shaggy **hair**.
Through the forests we'd **prowl**
With a **stomp** and a **growl**,

Then eat chips in his mountainous lair.

But Sister says a bear's too big,
And takes up half the bed.
She'd rather sleep with guinea pig
And scratch his fuzzy head.

But I don't want a fluffy pet
That sleeps for half the day,
I need a beast with lots of teeth
To play the games I play . . .

Like a **smoky** great dragon who **glows!**
And is **fierce** from his **horns** to his **toes!**

I would fly on his back,
And my sister attack

With a spout of red fire from his nose.

But Sister says I'm being silly,
That dragons don't exist.

She shows, instead, how guinea pigs
Go "chirrup" when they're kissed.

So soppy! Yuck! My sister's pet
Is not the pet for me.

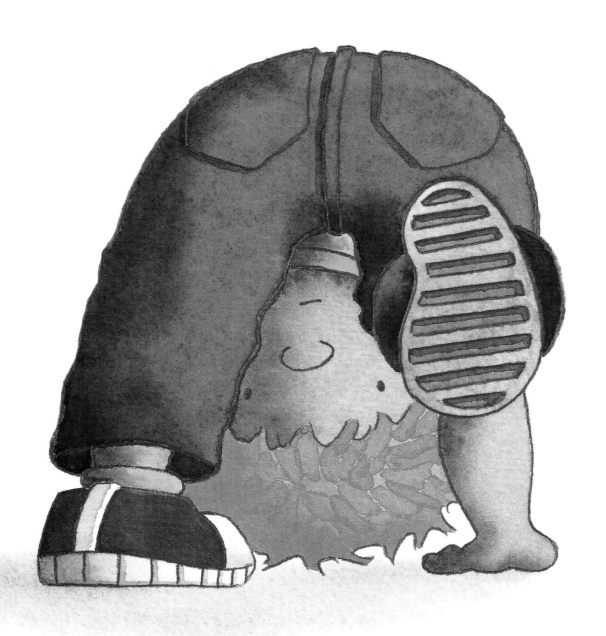

I'll show her all the pets you get –
I'll show her, then she'll see!

Like a **panther** with **big** padding **paws**.
Or a **polar** bear, **white** with black **claws**.
Or an **eagle**, or **rhino**,
Or huge roaring **dino**
With **great monster teeth** in his jaws!

Or a tentacled beast from the sea,
Or gorilla, or wild chimpanzee,
Or a snake, or a rat,
Or a sabre-toothed cat!
Oh, they'd all make such great pets for me!

But Sister smiles and rolls her eyes
And says that I will see
Just why she loves her guinea pig –
She pops him on my knee!

First he runs up my arm
with his claws,

Does a jump, and slides
down on his paws.
Then he curls in a ball

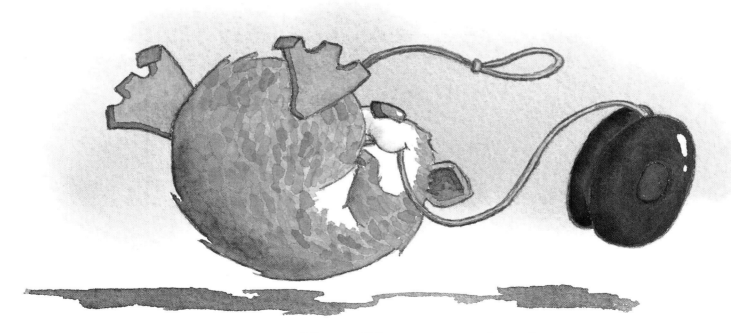

And rolls off down the hall,
And with one of my toys in his jaws!

So we chase him, and follow his squeak,
Try to get him wherever he peeks.

... over chairs,

Under rugs ...

We forget all our cares

Playing guinea pig's game:
hide-and-seek!

In the end I **agree** (but don't tell)
With my **sister** that **guineas** are **swell**.
If I say I won't **scare** him,
She **says** she will **share** him . . .